D1093556

SAN RAMON LIBRARY FOUNDATION

100 MONTGOMERY SAN RAMON, CALIFORNIA 94583

Put Beginning Readers on the Right Track with
ALL ABOARD READING™

The All Aboard Reading series is especially designed for beginning readers. Written by noted authors and illustrated in full color, these are books that children really want to read—books to excite their imagination, expand their interests, make them laugh, and support their feelings. With fiction and nonfiction stories that are high interest and curriculum-related, All Aboard Reading books offer something for every young reader. And with four different reading levels, the All Aboard Reading series lets you choose which books are most appropriate for your children and their growing abilities.

Picture Readers
Picture Readers have super-simple texts, with many nouns appearing as rebus pictures. At the end of each book are 24 flash cards—on one side is a rebus picture; on the other side is the written-out word.

Station Stop 1
Station Stop 1 books are best for children who have just begun to read. Simple words and big type make these early reading experiences more comfortable. Picture clues help children to figure out the words on the page. Lots of repetition throughout the text helps children to predict the next word or phrase—an essential step in developing word recognition.

Station Stop 2
Station Stop 2 books are written specifically for children who are reading with help. Short sentences make it easier for early readers to understand what they are reading. Simple plots and simple dialogue help children with reading comprehension.

Station Stop 3
Station Stop 3 books are perfect for children who are reading alone. With longer text and harder words, these books appeal to children who have mastered basic reading skills. More complex stories captivate children who are ready for more challenging books.

In addition to All Aboard Reading books, look for All Aboard Math Readers™ (fiction stories that teach math concepts children are learning in school); All Aboard Science Readers™ (nonfiction books that explore the most fascinating science topics in age-appropriate language); All Aboard Poetry Readers™ (funny, rhyming poems for readers of all levels); and All Aboard Mystery Readers™ (puzzling tales where children piece together evidence with the characters).

All Aboard for happy reading!

GROSSET & DUNLAP
Published by the Penguin Group
Penguin Group (USA) Inc., 375 Hudson Street, New York, New York 10014, U.S.A.
Penguin Group (Canada), 90 Eglinton Avenue East, Suite 700, Toronto, Ontario, Canada M4P 2Y3
(a division of Pearson Penguin Canada Inc.)
Penguin Books Ltd, 80 Strand, London WC2R 0RL, England
Penguin Ireland, 25 St Stephen's Green, Dublin 2, Ireland
(a division of Penguin Books Ltd)
Penguin Group (Australia), 250 Camberwell Road, Camberwell, Victoria 3124, Australia
(a division of Pearson Australia Group Pty Ltd)
Penguin Books India Pvt Ltd, 11 Community Centre, Panchsheel Park, New Delhi - 110 017, India
Penguin Group (NZ), Cnr Airborne and Rosedale Roads, Albany, Auckland 1310, New Zealand
(a division of Pearson New Zealand Ltd)
Penguin Books (South Africa) (Pty) Ltd, 24 Sturdee Avenue, Rosebank, Johannesburg 2196, South Africa

Penguin Books Ltd, Registered Offices:
80 Strand, London WC2R 0RL, England

ISBN 978-0-448-43952-5

10 9

ALL ABOARD READING™

PICTURE READER

MAX AND RUBY'S SHOW-AND-TELL

Based on the characters of
ROSEMARY WELLS

Grosset & Dunlap

Today is show-and-tell day

at Ruby's .

Ruby wants to

bake a .

She needs , ,

and  of

"U-Bake-It" instant cake.

Ruby's brother, ,

helps.

It takes many tries

to bake her .

Ruby picks up her .

 puts on his .

"No, Max.

You cannot come," says

 , walking out the .

"You are too young

to come to ."

 grabs a and ⬭

and goes outside.

"Yum, yum, yum,"

Max says, looking

at his 🍮 .

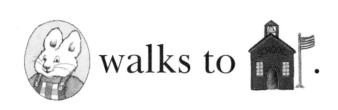 walks to 🏫.

Everyone is on the

playground.

Max swings on the

and slides down the .

He plays with a

big, red ⬤ .

When the  rings,

 goes inside.

He follows

to her classroom.

 finds an empty

at the back

of the classroom.

He sits down.

waits and waits.

There is a girl with a ,

a boy with a ,

and a girl with a .

Max yawns.

Next, it is 's turn.

Ruby gives out slices

of  .

Everyone likes Ruby's

 , especially .

"What do we have here?"

the teacher asks .

"Yum," says Max,

holding up his  .

"It looks so good,"

says the teacher.

"Let's put it

by the  ."

feels very proud.

 is so much fun!